SHORT TALES
Fairy Tales

# Beauty and the Beast

## Adapted by Christopher E. Long
## Illustrated by Mark Bloodworth

WAYLAND

# WAYLAND

First published in 2013 by Wayland

Copyright © 2013 Wayland

Wayland
338 Euston Road
London NW1 3BH

Wayland Australia
Level 17/207 Kent Street
Sydney, NSW 2000

Adapted Text by Christopher E. Long
Illustrations by Mark Bloodworth
Colours by Wes Hartman
Edited by Stephanie Hedlund
Interior Layout by Kristen Fitzner Denton and Alyssa Peacock
Book Design and Packaging by Shannon Eric Denton
Cover Design by Alyssa Peacock

Copyright © 2008 by Abdo Consulting Group

A cataloguing record for this title is available at the British Library.
Dewey number: 823.9'2

Printed in China

ISBN: 978 0 7502 7752 5

Wayland is a division of Hachette Children's Books, an Hachette UK company.
www.hachette.co.uk

There was once a very rich merchant.

He had six children.

He had three sons and three daughters.

All three daughters were very pretty.

But the youngest daughter was the prettiest.

Her name was Beauty.

Beauty's two older sisters were mean.

They teased their younger sister.

They were jealous of her beauty and kindness.

Many men asked the three sisters to marry them.

The two older sisters always said 'No!'

They wanted to marry a duke or an earl.

Beauty never wanted to be mean. So she always said that she was too young to marry.

One horrible day, Beauty's father lost all of his money.

He told his children that they must work.

The two older sisters yelled at their father.

'We will never get our hands dirty!' they cried.

The family moved to a farm. Beauty knew that she must make the best of things.

She worked hard to make life better for her family.

Her father and brothers worked in the fields.

Beauty cleaned and cooked.

But the two older sisters did nothing.

One day, Beauty's father left on business.

It started to snow.

The wind blew him off his horse twice.

He became lost in the forest.

The merchant lost all hope of seeing his children
again.

Out of nowhere, a great palace appeared.

Beauty's father decided to enter it for the night.

The next morning, he found the palace was full of wonders.

In his room, he found brand new clothes that fitted him perfectly.

When he went downstairs, he found a warm meal and hot chocolate. But no one was to be found.

'Thank you, magical palace, for giving me breakfast' he said.

He went outside to look for his horse.

The palace garden was not covered in snow,
and many beautiful flowers grew there.

Then, he saw the most beautiful red rose in the world.

He picked the red rose as a gift for Beauty.

Out of nowhere, a Beast appeared.

'I saved your life and you repay me by stealing my rose' the Beast growled.

'Please, I didn't mean to anger you' Beauty's father said.

'I picked this beautiful flower to give to my youngest daughter' he said.

'I will forgive you,' the Beast said, 'if you return in three months with one of your daughters.'

Beauty's father agreed.

All six children gathered around their father when he got home.

Beauty's father handed her the red rose.

'Take this flower, Beauty,' he said.

Beauty hugged her father as he cried.

'You will never know how much sadness this flower has brought me' he said.

He told his daughters that one of them must return to the Beast's palace.

Beauty's sisters yelled that they would not go.

Beauty told her father that she would go to the palace.

'I will not let you break your promise to the Beast'
Beauty said.

Three months later, Beauty rode off to the palace.

Her father cried as he watched her leave.

The horse took Beauty directly to the palace.

She was afraid, but she went inside.

A table was filled with wonderful food.

She ate and waited for the horrible Beast.

After dinner, a loud voice told Beauty to go upstairs.

She climbed the great staircase.

Beauty found a room with an open door.

Carefully, she went inside.

The room was beautiful.

It was a room for a princess.

She crawled into bed and cried herself to sleep.

The next morning, the Beast appeared in front of Beauty.

She was terrified of him.

'I can see that I frighten you,' the Beast said.

But Beauty asked the Beast to have breakfast with her.

Three months passed.

The Beast treated Beauty with kindness.

And Beauty and the Beast became friends.

They took long walks in the wonderful garden.

'I love you, Beauty' the Beast said. 'Is there anything I can do to make you happy?'

'Let me leave to see my father,' Beauty said. 'I miss him so.'

The Beast sadly agreed.

Beauty left the next day.

Upon arriving home, Beauty found that her sisters had married.

They made fun of Beauty for having to stay with the Beast.

'But I have come to love the Beast' Beauty said.

Beauty's sisters laughed at her.

'You had better marry him' her sisters said.

'Only a beast would take Beauty for a wife' they laughed.

That night, Beauty dreamed that the Beast was sick.

The next morning, Beauty rode back to the palace.

The Beast was dying of a broken heart.

'But I can die happy now that I have seen you again' the Beast said.

'You must not die. I cannot live without you!'
Beauty cried.

At that moment, the Beast magically changed.

He turned into a handsome prince.

The Prince told Beauty that a curse had turned him into the Beast.

Only true love could break the curse.

'I do love you' Beauty smiled.

The Prince asked Beauty to marry him.

'Of course I will marry you' she said.

Beauty's family was happy for her, except for her two sisters.

Beauty and the Prince had a grand wedding.

And they lived happily ever after.

# SHORT TALES
## Fables

### Titles in the Short Tales Fables series:

**The Ants and the Grasshopper**

978 0 7502 7756 3

**The Boy Who Cried Wolf**

978 0 7502 7757 0

**The Fox and the Grapes**

978 0 7502 7758 7

**The Lion and the Mouse**

978 0 7502 7783 9

**The Tortoise and the Hare**

978 0 7502 7784 6

**The Town Mouse and the Country Mouse**

978 0 7502 7785 3

## WAYLAND
www.waylandbooks.co.uk

Follow us on Twitter @waylandbooks | Find us on Facebook Wayland Books

# SHORT TALES
## Fairy Tales

Titles in the Short Tales Fairy Tales series:

### Aladdin and the Lamp

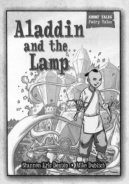

978 0 7502 7750 1

### Beauty and the Beast

978 0 7502 7752 5

### Jack and the Beanstalk

978 0 7502 7751 8

### Puss in Boots

978 0 7502 7754 9

### Sleeping Beauty

978 0 7502 7755 6

### The Little Mermaid

978 0 7502 7753 2

WAYLAND
www.waylandbooks.co.uk

Follow us on Twitter @waylandbooks | Find us on Facebook Wayland Books